llama llama loves camping

Anna Dewdney

Based on the bestselling children's book series
by Anna Dewdney

Penguin Young Readers Licenses
An Imprint of Penguin Random House

PENGUIN YOUNG READERS LICENSES
An Imprint of Penguin Random House LLC

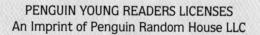

ISBN 9781524787189

16 15 14 13 12

"I'm excited to go camping tomorrow!" Llama Llama tells his friends. He has never camped overnight before. Neither has Nelly Gnu, Luna, Gilroy, or Euclid.

"It will be super fun," Mama Llama says. "And Grandma Llama and I will be with you the whole time."

"Camping is going to be very different from being at home," says Llama.

Luna nods. "We'll be out in the open, under the trees and sky."

"And we won't have any kitchen or house things, like a refrigerator, an oven, or lights," says Gilroy.

Euclid looks worried. After all, he loves gadgets. "We can't use any machines while we camp?" he asks.

"That's right," says Mama Llama. "We are just going to bring the essentials. *Essentials* are the few things we really need. But don't worry, Euclid. It's only for one day and night!"

The next day is warm and sunny as the campers arrive at the campground. "Welcome to our overnight adventure in the woods!" says Grandma Llama.

Llama Llama and his friends cheer loudly.

Everyone has one bag, except for Euclid. He's carrying two!

"Don't worry," he explains. "I only brought the essentials."

"That's a lot of essentials!" Nelly says with a laugh.

"Okay, campers," says Mama Llama. "Let's go for a hike while it's still light outside!"

Euclid pulls a handheld gadget out of one of his bags. "I can plug our route into my directional device," he says.

"Remember, Euclid," Llama says kindly, "no gadgets allowed."

Euclid sighs. "Okay," he says, putting it away. "Not using gadgets isn't going to be easy!"

Mama Llama leads the campers along a trail in the woods.

"Wow," says Llama, looking around. "These trees are so tall!"

"I wonder how tall they are," Euclid says.

"Can I measure them with my digital tape measure?"

Luna shakes her head. "No gadgets," she reminds him.

"Oh, yeah," Euclid says.

When the group gets farther into the woods, Mama Llama asks the campers to stop for a moment. "Let's listen to the sounds of nature," she says. "What do you hear?"

Llama pauses. "I hear a bird chirping," he says.

"I hear leaves rustling," says Luna.

"I hear a tree creaking," says Gilroy.

Nelly points to a bee. "I hear him buzzing," she says.

"I hear all that, too," says Euclid. "And I hear water flowing in the distance."

"The sounds in the woods are very different from the sounds at home," says Luna.

"Yeah," says Nelly. "Those are machine sounds. *Beep! Ring, ring! Wee-ooo, wee-ooo!*" She laughs at her imitation of a siren.

Euclid pulls a tape recorder and a camera from his bag. "I want to make a recording to remember the sounds," he explains.

Mama Llama smiles at Euclid. "For this trip, let's just listen hard to remember everything," she says.

"I forgot," says Euclid. "This no-gadgets thing is tougher than I thought."

After their hike, Llama and his friends help Mama Llama and Gram set up camp. Instead of a house, they have a tent. Instead of a refrigerator, they have a cooler with ice. And instead of an oven, they have a roaring campfire!

"It takes some work to camp out," says Mama Llama. "But it helps you appreciate the nice things you have at home a little more."

Later, the campers eat a delicious dinner around the fire. "And now it's time for dessert!" says Grandma Llama, handing out sticks.

"Do we just eat these?" asks Gilroy.

"No," says Gram, laughing. "You eat these marshmallows after we roast them in the fire!"

As the sun sets, everyone roasts marshmallows over the fire. They taste delicious—even better than a dessert you make at home!

"It's getting pretty dark out," says Nelly.

"It is," says Euclid. "But it's pretty nice roasting marshmallows in nature," he adds. "With no gadgets!"

Finally, it's time for bed. Inside the tent, the campers get cozy in their sleeping bags. Once they're all tucked in, Mama Llama has an idea.

"Let's listen closely to the sounds outside and pretend they're music," she says.

The campers close their eyes. They hear crickets chirping. They hear a bird calling. They hear the wind whooshing and an owl hooting.

"It sounds like they're all talking to each other," says Llama. The music of the forest is very peaceful. As they listen to the nighttime sounds, the campers slowly drift off to sleep.

In the morning, sunlight streams into the tent. The campers wake up feeling refreshed. Mama Llama and Gram are very proud of Llama and his friends for spending the entire night in the woods.

But everyone is especially proud of Euclid. "Good job!" cheers Llama Llama. "You didn't use any gadgets on our campout!"

"Thank you," Euclid says. "It was a fun challenge. I like the woods!" The other campers agree.

"Can we go on another hike before we leave?" Nelly asks.

"We sure can," says Grandma Llama. "But first, breakfast!"

"We can use my electric waffle maker!" says Euclid. "Oh, wait," he adds. "That's kind of a gadget, isn't it?" He's made it this far without using machines. He isn't going to stop now!